For Pete, Isaac, and Lily
with deepest love

Published in 2004 in the United States by Ragged Bears
413 Sixth Avenue
Brooklyn, New York 11215
www.raggedbears.com

Originally published in 2003 in Great Britain by Ragged Bears
Milborne Wick, Sherborne, Dorset DT9 4PW

First American Edition
Printed in China
ISBN 1-929927-53-3
2 4 6 8 10 9 7 5 3 1

Lovely Ruby
and the Mermaid

By Nancy Trott

RAGGED BEARS

Brooklyn, New York • Milborne Wick, Dorset

Lovely Ruby is my best friend ever!
She used to live near me in the city —
but now she has moved to the seaside.
Ruby says that the waves tickle her toes
and make her miss me.

I say, "I miss you too, Ruby."

Ruby's new house is high on a hill.
She says she can hear the sound of the sea
as she sits in her bedroom thinking of me.

Ruby sends me letters and packages
full of things she finds by the sea.

One morning, Ruby was walking on the beach when she saw the loveliest shell she had ever seen.

And when she took a closer look,
she noticed a strand —
a golden strand that glistened
and sparkled in the sun.

What could it be?

Ruby knew just what it was!
It was a golden strand
of mermaid's hair.

Now Ruby says we shouldn't tell —
she has a new friend and she's magical, too!

Ruby's mermaid friend lives beneath the sea in a dreamland of blue, beyond the deep.

Ruby says, when she's asleep,
she hears the mermaid whispering –
whispers about magical princesses
in underwater worlds.

Mermaid whispers make such happy dreams.

And when Ruby wakes again
she finds a treasure from the sea.
It was left for her by her mermaid friend —
a precious gift to make her smile.

The mermaid knows Ruby is missing me.

Then, **SPLASH**,
the mermaid is gone again,
back into her waterland.

And when I open the package tied up
with string that Ruby has sent to me,
there is the shell —
the loveliest shell I have ever seen.

The mermaid had left it for Ruby
and Ruby has sent it to me.

Lovely Ruby is my best friend ever —
Lovely Ruby by the sea.

A Poem for Ruby

Lovely Ruby by the sea
sent a precious gift to me.
A shell she found upon the sand,
and in it was a golden strand.
A golden strand of mermaid hair,
from Ruby's friend who lives somewhere...
beneath the blue, beyond the deep.
She talks to Ruby in her sleep
then leaves her treasures on the sand
and dives back into her waterland.
And Ruby sent her gift to me...
...lovely Ruby by the sea.